Phineas in Africa:
The Sudan

by

Elizabeth Chapin-Pinotti

A Phineas J. Clooney Adventure: Book 3

1

Note for Librarians: a cataloguing record for this book that includes Dewey Decimal
Classification and US Library of Congress numbers is available from the Library and
Archives of Canada. The complete cataloguing record can be obtained from their
online database at: www.collectionscanada.ca/amicus/index-e.html
ISBN 1-4120-3919-3

TRAFFORD

Offices in Canada, USA, Ireland, UK and Spain
This book was published *on-demand* in cooperation with Trafford Publishing.
On-demand publishing is a unique process and service of making a book available
for retail sale to the public taking advantage of on-demand manufacturing and
Internet marketing. On-demand publishing includes promotions, retail sales,
manufacturing, order fulfilment, accounting and collecting royalties on behalf of the
author.
Book sales for North America and international:
Trafford Publishing, 6E–2333 Government St.,
Victoria, BC v8t 4p4 CANADA
phone 250 383 6864 (toll-free 1 888 232 4444)
fax 250 383 6804; email to orders@trafford.com
Books sales in Europe:
Trafford Publishing (uk) Ltd., Enterprise House, Wistaston Road Business Centre,
Wistaston Road, Crewe, Cheshire cw2 7rp UNITED KINGDOM
phone 01270 251 396 (local rate 0845 230 9601)
facsimile 01270 254 983; orders.uk@trafford.com
Order online at:
www.trafford.com/robots/04-1727.html

10 9 8 7 6 5 4 3

For Steven P.

The Beginning

Or...required reading if you missed Away: Book 1

It all began on my twelfth birthday. See, I was kind of bummed because my Grandfather Clooney couldn't make it out to California for my party. This was the first time ever. Grandpa Clooney lives in Massachusetts and owns the oldest candy factory in the United States. It is an historical landmark and was even used as a hospital in both the Revolutionary and Civil Wars. He sent me a present. Of course I'd rather have Grandpa and no present but this particular present is rather intriguing. Intriguing is a fancy smancy word I just learned for mysterious.

My present came brightly wrapped and with instructions that I could only open it in the presence of two other Explorers. No one else! Which is why I am, not so patiently, sitting on my bed, staring at my present waiting for Katie and Jeff to arrive. I chose Katie and Jeff because, well Katie is my best friend and Jeff is my second best friend. Also, I sort of have a tiny bit of a crush on Jeff – of course I would positively die if anyone, even Katie, knew about it. So there you go. Katie and Jeff. Jeff and Katie...*late* Jeff and Katie.

In mid-thought I hear a rap at my window. Finally!

"I thought the cake wasn't until six. What gives?" Jeff asks as he hurdles my second story window and tackles my bed.

"This better be important. It's cutting into crucial gift buying time." Katie adds.

"Why don't you already *have* my present?" I tease my best friend.

"Because you are absolutely impossible to shop for." She smiles as Jeff picks up my brightly colored box.

"So this is the big surprise." He shakes the box and tosses it to me. "I wonder what it is?"

I briefed them both over the phone and now I tear into it. "Ok, Grandpa...here we go." I open the wrapping to reveal a silver box.

"It looks like a hand held computer." Katie says.

"It does. Cool." I say opening the box. "I wonder what the big deal about opening it is." I pick up the computer and it starts to rumble. It sounds like it is clearing its throat.

"Whoa..." Jeff says as he moves in closer to get a better look. "That's the big deal. It's alive."

"Don't be silly Jeff," Katie adds, "it can't be alive." Grandpa's picture comes on the screen. "Wow! I guess it kind of is alive."

"Grandpa!" I screech excitedly as his face appears on the screen.

"Happy Birthday Phineas. Sorry, I couldn't be there in person." My grandpa smiles. His picture is crystal clear and in color.

"Wow, Grandpa...this is too awesome!" I say.

"Just wait and you will really know awesome. Put me on the desk Phineas and the three of you sit down. I assume Jeff is there somewhere." Jeff comes into view and waves. "Ah, there he is...hello Jeff."

"How'd you know Jeff was here, Grandpa?" I ask.

"Who else would you pick, Phineas, besides Miss Katie and Master Jeff?"

I shrug. "You've got a point there."

"Now, the three of you sit right in front of the monitor so I can see you. See the blue lens?" We all squint closer to see what Grandpa is talking about. "That's the camera."

"Way cool!"

"Now, stand back." Grandpa says. "And hold on to your hats."

We stand back and instantaneously Grandpa is in the room with us. No smoke, no mirrors, no loud ka-boom and no LIE...Grandpa materializes...just like that. None of us can speak. My grandfather just laughs and pulls me in for a hug. "Phineas, my girl, welcome to the next age of modems."

"Holy cow!" Jeff says as he touches my grandpa to make certain that he is real. "You beamed yourself to us!"

"Wow!" Katie says softly as she also touches Grandpa.

"Wait until I tell the others," Jeff says with eyes still as big as saucers, "they'll completely flip!"

"Whoa, Jeff my boy, there'll be no telling others. Only you three," Grandpa says as he sits on my bed. "Gather round girls and boys I've got some explaining to do."

"No, really, Grandpa...how'd you get here? The closet? Under the bed?" I ask, too stunned to believe he could actually transport himself via modem.

"There's a lot about me that you don't know children. There's a lot I'm not certain that you are ready to hear, but they think you are, so here goes."

"It all started," Grandpa begins, "when your great, great, great, great, great, great Grandpa Clooney started the Clooney Candy Factory as a front for pre-Revolutionary War era spies."

"The Candy Factory was a front for spies...cool." Jeff says.

"Still is...only the spy game has changed a bit in the past few years." Grandpa adds.

"Grandpa," I say – beginning to understand, "you mean to tell me that you are a spy?"

"Like all the Clooneys were before me." Grandpa says proudly. "We've worked for the government of this United States before there was a government here to work for."

"And, Dad?" I ask not really believing that my father could actually be a spy. Grandpa...maybe...he's the type...adventurous, spontaneously, meticulous and always off to some exotic location...but Dad...he's so...normal.

"Your father was one of the best, but he quit to coach soccer when you joined AYSO." Grandpa shakes his head. "A great loss," he pauses and looks at us closely. "Anyway, as I said, the spy game has changed and it is about to involve all of you...if you are willing."

"Us? Spies? Again...way cool!" Katie, my shy best friend, says.

"You hate adventure," I say looking at Katie, "if there was a caption in the yearbook that read 'least likely to be a spy' your picture would be right above it!"

Grandpa pats Katie's leg. "It's always the shy ones Phin, they're the best."

"So when's our first assignment?" Katie asks.

Jeff picks up the handheld computer. "Do we get to use the modem?"

Grandpa takes the computer. "Let's not get ahead of ourselves," he says. "We've got a lot of work to do."

We each take turns "moding" ourselves to the candy factory. It's really very easy. Push the icon shaped like a map, type in your location and poof...you're there...literally. It happens so fast that it doesn't even hurt. It gets Katie a little motion sick but other than that...nothing. When we are all at the candy factory grandpa leads us to a huge briefing room and begins explaining.

"As I said before," Grandpa starts, "the spy game has changed over the past few years. The days of James Bond fighting the evil "Red" empire that was the USSR is over."

"What's the USSR?" Jeff asks.

"The USSR was a huge country made up of Russia and a lot of those other little Eastern European countries. It was under Communist rule for a long time. The United States and the USSR basically divided up the world. Some countries were behind the "Red" iron curtain and others were free, like us." Katie impresses us with her historical knowledge.

Grandpa smiles at Katie. "Very good Katie. The spy game was big then – with both powers, superpowers we called them, capable of leveling the earth with nuclear weaponry, each side needed to know what was going on with the other. But with the break up of Communism we've shifted our focus and are concentrating on more humanitarian efforts."

"We sound perfect," I smile excitedly.

"So they think," my grandfather refers to this "they" again, "but I'm not so sure. You are so young."

"Who is 'they' and what exactly do these 'they' people want us to do?" I ask.

"'They' are on a need to know basis and I'm getting to your assignment." Grandpa pats my hand. "As you are probably aware the world is not such a nice place for lots of people, lots of children, to live."

"It's horrible!" Katie says, "children working in factories, fighting in wars, abducted or worse!" Abducted is one of Katie's college words that means stolen or kidnapped.

"Exactly. That's where we come in," Grandpa continues. "We are on a mission to promote and secure global tolerance and 'they' feel that the only way that this will be achieved is through the children of the world. By educating the children of the world on issues of basic human rights and freedom, by teaching them tolerance and showing them that we are all, indeed, created equal, 'they' feel that global peace can finally be achieved. Basically, we are teaching the leaders of tomorrow to know and understand each other. Hopefully, by personally knowing people and then knowing about people and places outside of the sheltered box we live in, tolerance and therefore peace can more easily be attained."

"Like that'll ever happen," Jeff says. "Even if we all, us kids I mean, become educated and join forces we won't have any real power until we are older anyway. What can three kids do?"

"I am not a 'kid' – I am an adolescent," Katie corrects.

"Ok, two kids and an *adolescent*!" Jeff rolls his eyes. "My point remains the same."

"Your mission is to bring together more than three. You are to transmodulate, via modem, to designated countries and rescue children in crisis. These children will be transmodulated back here and work with you three by serving on the new International Coalition of Children for Peace. This council will act as a junior United Nations if you will. A global body to obtain, monitor and insure tolerance and peace by making people aware of such global issues."

By global issues I'm pretty sure that Grandpa is talking about the way the world is now and all of the bad things in it. Wow, it's amazing that he and 'they' feel that we, kids of all people, are capable of something so grand.

15

But why not? Grown-ups have been trying to achieve the peace and humanity thing for, what?...ever...and it really isn't working. I think their problem, the grown-ups I mean, is that they can't see peace or progress unless they change all of the other people into mini-versions of themselves.

As Grandpa keeps talking I realize that 'they' think that we kids can succeed because we are not demanding anything and that we will be more comfortable letting the people of other countries live the way they want to – as long as it is fair for all of citizens in these countries.

"But Phineas, you must remember...all of you must remember. You may be rescuing these others out of situations that are horrendous; however, you are no better than they are. You must not fall into the trap that some aid workers or other people in positions of "rescuing" fall into to – the trap of thinking you are better than they are because you happen to be helping them out of a bad situation. Phineas, you and your Explorer friends were chosen, because we do not believe you will act this way."

"Of course not Grandpa," I say – a little overwhelmed by the morning's events.

"The people you will be bringing back here are smart and were hand-picked to sit on the international coalition I told you about. They are as bright as you and have just as much to offer. Together you will be the hope for peace. Never forget that."

"Got it," Jeff said.

Katie and I nod. Grandpa smiles back at us.

This sounds like a pretty big order to fill...but I'm ready. By the gleam in Jeff's eyes and the smile on Katie's entire face I think that they are ready too.

Chapter 1

I'm Phineas J. Clooney and I'm going to be a city planner. You know, the person behind how a city looks. I'm going to design beautiful buildings with lots of parks and water gardens. The center of every Clooney creation will be a main street exactly like the one at Disneyland. Maybe I'll even put a castle at the end of each main street. Sort of like a gateway to the city. I, of course, will stay in the castle whenever I am visiting each of my cities.

Today, however, I'm a secret agent of sorts. It all started when my Grandpa Clooney couldn't make it to my birthday last month and sent me a present instead. The present turned out to be one of those life-changing gifts, and not just for me, but for my best friend Katie and my second best friend Jeff too.

The present was a hand held computer.
A very high tech hand held computer capable of
modeming a human being, actually three or
four human beings, as easily as it can a
picture. It's called transmodulating. This is a
top-secret spy gadget that was created by the
United States government to aid in the rescue
of children and in the salvation of the earth.

All my life I thought that my sweet, jolly
Grandpa Clooney was merely the owner of the
oldest candy factory in the United States. On
this life-changing birthday, however, I found
out that he is actually a spy and that the candy
factory is really a cover for an intricate secret
agent organization. Intricate means very
complicated or spider web like. I learned it on
The Game Show Network.

It turns out that all of the Clooneys now,
and all of the Clooneys who ever came before
us, have worked or do work for the US

Government in cooperation with a global peace organization called "Help Our World". Cooperation means to work with someone without fighting or anything and global means including everyone and everything in the whole wide world. Or everyone and everything around the globe...get it...globe, global.

On this last birthday of mine, Grandpa Clooney decided that it was time for me to join in the Clooney tradition so he made me an official agent. He also included my two best friends: Katie and Jeff.

Which brings me to now – and why the three of us are sitting in my room, on my bed, waiting for our second assignment. It's rather comical exactly how we are sitting...all in a row...staring at the floating Windows logo on an otherwise black computer screen.

We are way excited. Our first mission was extremely successful. We went to this country in Africa, called Sierra Leone, and brought back an orphaned girl named Saramba for the International Coalition of Children for Peace – a new organization we are forming. That's the purpose of our secret agenting – bringing back kids from countries where bad things are happening and then forming a group of kids to help fix the world.

By fixing the world we don't mean that we're going to try to make everybody exactly like us. How boring would that be! By fixing the world we mean using us kids to figure out how we can work together to get along. We are not trying to turn the world into mini-America's, but rather, we are trying to make sure that nobody goes to bed hungry, that nobody is kidnapped and forced to work when they don't want to, and that the world is safe for everyone to be exactly who he or she wants to be – so long as who he or she wants to be doesn't hurt anyone else.

This is what they told us anyway. But to tell you the truth – I think there are deeper things at work here. So deep that they may be beyond what the grown-ups can understand.

See, I have an idea about this peace thing. It stems from Mrs. Vandenberg's fourth grade classroom. Whenever kids weren't getting along – she'd force them to sit together with a couple of other kids until they figured out their differences. We also did all sorts of projects to show how the same even different people can be. She explained to us how – one on one – people usually get along. I think that we will be able to get closer to peace because we will be meeting kids and liking them beyond the flags of their country. Someday I'm going to tell Grandpa that this coalition of his needs to be more than twenty hand selected kids –

but full of regular kids from all over the world. Anyway...

Our trip into Sierra Leone was scary at first. Actually, I wasn't sure we'd even make it out. We were chased, captured, tricked and held at gunpoint. And that was only in the first hour. Not your average day for an American junior high kid – but then we are anything but average.

Especially Jeff. He the opposite of average. If average was the sun, then Jeff would be the moon. If average was water, then Jeff would be the desert. If average was a storm, then Jeff would be the sunshine. In case you haven't noticed, I've recently developed a little bit of a crush on Jeff. Emphasis on the word secret. I would die if anyone, including Katie, ever found out. See, I'm Phineas J. Clooney – tough, smart, nice and ever so cute – tomboy girl. And tough, smart, nice and ever so cute – tomboy girl – Phineas does not get crushes. Phineas saves the world.

That's why my friends and I founded this group called the Explorers. We "explore" the community searching for nice things to do for people and then we do them. We collect toys at Christmas, help feed the homeless, read to small children, visit "shut-ins" living in Eastwood Retirement Community – things like that. Now we've branched off on this secret agent thing.

"Buzzzz, whirrrl." The transmodulator pixels to life. "Sputter, crackle." And instantly Grandpa Clooney appears on the screen.

"Grandpa!" Even his image being broadcast thousands of miles, from Massachusetts to California, makes me excited. I love being with my Grandpa.

"Why, hello, Phineas," Grandpa smiles his biggest grin, "Jeff, Katie."

"Hey, Mr. Clooney," Jeff waves.

"Hi, Grandpa Clooney," Katie charms. "How's Saramba?"

"Fine, fine. She's living with a young couple from a town near her's. They're trying to find out if any of her family is still alive."

"That's so cool!" Jeff says.

"When can we see her again?" I ask.

"Soon, soon," Grandpa says in that repeating way he has. "After your next mission. And, speaking of which...how do you feel about another trip to the great African continent?"

"Sure," I say. "Why not?"

"Which part?" Katie asks the obvious question.

"Ever heard of the Sudan?"

"Wow!" Jeff's eye gleam reappears. "Hey, I heard on the radio that the Sudan is on the list of countries where they still sell people into slavery."

Shocked, our eyes immediately shift to Jeff.

"And they said this on 102.5 – *the pumpin' sound of today*?" I ask sarcastically. Jeff does not listen to stations that would give him information on global situations.

"Public radio." He states.

This time I blink back my surprise.

"My mom." He assures.

"Actually," Katie begins, "the Sudan is known for a great many things, including an active slave trade. Did you know that there is a group of traders, called Mujahedin in the Nuba Mountains and Janjaweed in the Darfur Region, who set fire to villages so that they can steal the women and children and sell them into slavery? Today! Now! This century. While we are at the movies or roaming the mall

or whining because we have to go to school –
thousands of tribal people are being kidnapped
and sold into slavery."

How does she know everything, I wonder.

"It's about selling people and taking land
and one group thinking they are better than
the African's who live there."

"Right you are Katie." Grandpa Clooney
shakes his head. "That's why you are going to
the Nuba Mountains. You are looking for a
young boy named Babo. He lives near a village
called Kodi. He is a bright boy who wants to be
a doctor and then go back and work with his
people. He speaks three languages – and one
of them is English." Grandpa's face suddenly
grows more serious than I have ever seen it.
"This is a very dangerous region. There are
dangerous people and it is landmined."

"Bummer," Jeff whispers.

"You must pay careful attention to the map on the transmodulator. It contains a detailed layout of where we think the landmines are."

"Think?" I interrupt. "Grandpa, I'm your only granddaughter. You adore me. Can't you find a map that more than thinks it has all of the landmines labeled?"

"I would if I could, Phineas my dear, I would if I could." He shakes his head again. "This is only one hazard. When one such land mine blew-up and eight people were killed – the government decided that it was going to stop the organization in charge of clearing the mines. This was also the organization that was doing the most to help the cease-fire along."

"A cease-what?" Jeff asks.

"A cease-fire. It's an agreement between two countries or two groups of people who are warring with each other to stop fighting so that

they can try to talk through their problems."
Katie states.

I even know that one.

"Right you are Katie. This is the second
reason that the area is so dangerous...the
cease-fire is on very shaky grounds."

"No pun intended." We all look at Jeff.
"Get it, landmines, shaky ground."

"Anyway," Grandpa continues, ignoring
my pal's attempt at humor.

"You gotta keep your sense of humor,"
Jeff mumbles.

He really is adorable. But I, Phineas J.
Clooney, would rather eat live tarantulas than
admit I think anyone – especially Jeff – is
adorable!

"You will find no humor in landmines
Jeff. Especially if you stumble upon one."
Grandpa finishes his briefing with a sad look
shadowing his eyes. When he flickers out of

the transmodulator, the shadows now loom in all of our eyes. Loom is a fluffy word that means to appear. I'm using it because it just sounds more dangerous and I have a feeling that life is about to get more than a little more dangerous for me and my three best friends.

Chapter 2

Grandpa's face flickers to black, the floating Windows logo reappears, and Jeff and Katie leave to gather their things. We will meet back in my room in exactly one hour and then we are off to the Sudan.

I'm ready, so I fire up the transmodulator and research the country to which we are going. The boy we are to meet is named Babo. His family was killed in a raid and now he lives with one of the village elders. He is smart and attends an Arab school. He used to go to a Christian school but the missionaries were chased out by the government that is centered in the country's capital city of Khartoum.

There is no electricity in the Nuba Mountains, so he studies by kerosene lamp light. He is our age, wears a uniform and walks miles to school everyday. The uniform pants, shirt and shoes he wears are the first real clothes he's ever had on.

I, Phineas J. Clooney, would not like that. I, Phineas J. Clooney, would get very cold and be very embarrassed if I had to run around naked all the time. Besides, what a sunburn I'd get.

Grandpa said Babo knows we are coming. This world of secret agents is so different from the movies. I mean in the movies we would swoop down and rescue people unannounced. Today, it seems announcements are sent! Not really – but just about.

See, Babo met some of Grandpa's friends who were scouting in the Nuba Mountains, learned about the council and asked to join. Those people, the friends of Grandpa Clooney's, were going to take him back, but they were killed in what Grandpa called a skirmish between friendlies. I'm not all that sure what a skirmish is but I don't think being shot to death can ever be considered friendly.

The Nuba Mountains are actually more like hills that jump right out of the flat plains of Africa. They are rocky, but things grow well there. I guess you can say they are farmable – if farmable's a word that is. Anyway, this farmability is a good thing because the people who live in the Nuba Mountains usually suffer less from those droughts when the rain doesn't come and food can't grow and animals die. This is a bad thing because other people, outsiders, like this fertile area. Fertile means that lots of things grow there. Fertile areas are farmable and in a land of mostly deserts – fertile is a sought after thing.

A tap, tap, tapping at my window interrupts my research. I look out. Jeff and Katie are scaling the rose lattice up to my second story room. I wonder if my parents though at all about putting climbing roses on lattice outside the window of a Phineas J. Clooney, like myself. I mean, it's exactly as if there's a ladder directly to my room. Don't my parents know me and my friends well enough to know that a few rose thorns will not keep me or them from climbing up and down the wall instead of using the door?

"Hey, Phineas. All set!" Jeff sounds excited.

Once again, Katie looks green.

"Do you have the remote belt?" Katie asks.

I lift up my T-shirt and show them the not-so-stylish belt that Grandpa demands I wear at all times when traveling. See, if the transmodulator is not attached to me constantly, either in my hands or by this remote, then I won't be able to escape if we get into trouble.

One of the reasons that my parents actually let me take on such a tough and dangerous job is this remote. Jeff and Katie each have a tiny remote device that will transmodulate them whenever I push the little blue button – providing they are in range. We have an extra remote for whoever we happen to be picking up.

The actual transmodulator-computer thingy can transport up to three people, besides me, if we are all touching it. It can also act like a remote, but it has way limited range. The limited range and touching things might not always be practical. Like, for example, if I'm getting shot at and Jeff is being hauled away by angry preventers of peace and Katie is hiding so she won't get captured...well, if I push the button, yippee for me, but my friends spend the next decade or so in some dark, foreign prison...eating nothing but dry bread and drinking dirty water. So, we have these remotes as our safety net.

Funny, this is our second trip and all and I should be getting used to it...but these tiny pieces of plastic do not make me feel so very safe.

Another thing that does not make me feel so very safe is the loss of power. What if we are in the middle of nowhere, snakes are crawling through the trees, leaches are digging into our skin, bad people are closing in...and the cell phone thing happens? You know the "can you hear me now" connection loss? When there is no signal. What if we get no signal?

Before we went to Sierra Leone Grandpa explained about this bacterium battery, planted in the transmodulator, that can't run out of juice. He claims that there are certain strains of bacteria...you know the thing that makes people sick...that can't be destroyed and that multiply at such fast rates that the energy they produce can power an entire computer for, like, ever.

Can you imagine what would happen if such a bacteria escaped from the battery and fell into the wrong hands? Or if the bacteria caught a different bacteria and died right in the middle of a transmodulation?

Normally, I don't question my Grandpa Clooney...but this time...

Grandpa's voice breaks my thoughts, as the transmodulator rumbles to life.

"Afternoon travelers! Are you ready for your journey?" Grandpa is smiling but I can tell he's more nervous than we are.

"Absolutely!" Jeff jumps from my bed and faces the screen.

Katie hugs her backpack straps tightly to her. "I suppose."

"Again, children I wish you luck. I am confident you will be successful. Babo is waiting for you. This one should be easy."

Should. I learned a long time ago that if something should be anything – it never is!

"Just push the red button if you need me Phineas, and I'll be right with you."

"Bye, Grandpa! I love you." I say as Grandpa fades to gray.

"Good-bye kids. Bye Phineas. I love you, too. Remember, watch for landmines and raiders." And he is out.

"Raiders? What raiders?" I ask, but it is too late.

I grab my backpack. Jeff does the same. Katie pulls her straps even tighter.

I touch the transmodulator.

Katie touches the transmodulator.

Jeff touches the transmodulator.

I look at Katie and then at Jeff. I hold my breath, close my eyes and push the blue button.

Chapter 3

We land exactly where the transmodulator is programmed. The screen says that we are in the Nuba Mountains, Sudan, Africa. We are actually on a beautiful hill.

If I look to my left I see jagged mountains that lead up to flat landings, like steps cut into a gigantic rock. There are lots of trees, black dirt and boulders.

If I look to my right I see flat, golden red land. For miles and miles there is nothing but a golden red sea of grass that seems to touch the brilliant blue horizon at the end of forever. A single scrubby tree dots the waving land. It really does look like water, waving in the slight breeze that doesn't do much to break the heat of the African sun.

Africa. We are in Africa again. Numbers blink on the bottom of the screen: geographic coordinates 15 00 N 30 00 E.

Again, I make a mental note to pay closer attention in Mr. Felding's geography class because I still have no idea what those numbers really mean. I remember the double "l" words – you know – longitude and latitude. But that's about it.

"I guess we're here." Katie says brushing off her shorts and relacing her hiking boots.

"Man, it's hot!" Jeff bounces up and grins out over the plains. "Not ordinary hot...but Africa hot! Hey, I wonder how many lions are laying in that grass down there?"

"Nice happy thought." I look out over the plain then to Katie. She is looking a little green. "You OK?" I ask.

"I took a motion sickness pill. It didn't work." She wipes her glasses and her forehead with her long sleeved T-shirt.

"You wanna rest a minute?" I ask my buddy.

"No, I want to find Babo and go home." She states matter-of-factly.

Jeff looks up the mountain and then over the plain again. "Don't suppose there is any way around going up?"

"Grandpa said the Nuba Mountains...not the Nuba Plains."

"It's a desert not a plain." Katie corrects. "And, according to the map, Babo's village is at the end of this trail." She moves her finger to follow a trail that leads to the blinking blue light that is us on the screen. You know, kind of like the "You Are Here" label on a map.

"Up the trail," I lead.

Jeff is behind me, carrying the transmodulator with the blinking, moving, "You Are Here", light. Katie is close behind him.

"Stay to your right Phineas." Jeff cautions.

I remember the landmines and the Nuba Mountains suddenly aren't so pretty anymore.

"They're mostly down there." Jeff points back down to the desert plains. "But they are along the smoother trial up there too."

I slowly take two steps backwards and begin up the other trail. "Figures," I mumble as I begin to weave up the thin, winding path.

This walk to the village twists through rocks and trees. We are past the landmines and now these Nuba Mountains seem less dangerous than Sierra Leone. They seem more peaceful. Only, like I said before, whenever something seems anything – it's usually the opposite.

After about a half hour or so, we come to a village that is backed up against a huge rock. The rock forms a canopy that seems to drape over mud huts. High above the rock the hills have turned to mountains and these mountains seem to reach the sky.

We hide in the bushes – surveying our new surroundings.

"The transmodulator says we're here," Jeff whispers – only Jeff doesn't whisper very well. A little boy walking by, probably six or so, turns towards us. I freeze. I don't even dare breathe. I guess he doesn't see us, looses interest and goes back to his playing.

"See those compounds," Katie points to one of the little square fenced-off areas. There are several of them. Each has two or three huts facing each other. The fences are regular wooden posts but they are filled in with straw. It reminds me of the first little piggy's house.

The one made of straw. "Those are called shal's. Families live in them. The huts are like bedrooms and living rooms. They're sort of like our houses, but since it's so warm they don't need to be connected by hallways."

"How do you always know this stuff?" Jeff asks.

Katie just smiles and points back to the shal. "One of the huts is called the holua. This is where the unmarried boys eat and sleep together. The dad sleeps with the mother and children in one of the huts, usually the largest, but he eats with the unmarried boys. The Nuba are extremely friendly. They share any meal with whoever is around at the time. Anyone who is within hearing distance is welcome."

"We are going to stick out like sore thumbs." I state. Looking around I notice no sign of western clothing. I also notice no light colored people.

"Yes, but no." Once again, Katie is going to provide us with answers. "There are some missionaries here or there used to be. They've seen people like us wander through before. The missionary thing in always a good cover, because those people are always wandering around in harms way!"

"Saved our butts once," Jeff smiles.

"Thank God for missionaries," I giggle. "Get it? Missionaries are religious. Thank God for them."

Jeff rolls his eyes. Katie ignores my comments and continues.

No sense of humor. Mental note, find funnier friends.

"Also, during times when there is no rain and then no food – aid workers come in with provisions. So, while white people are rare –

they are a sign of good things...mostly.
Besides, according to Nuba custom, it would be
impolite to point out our differences."

"You keep saying "Nuba" – like they are
one people. I thought there were lots of
different tribes out here?" I ask.

"There are, but lots of customs and rules
are the same from tribe to tribe." Katie adds.

"Oh," I respond.

Jeff points to a clearing. There appears
to be a boxing or wrestling ring of sorts set up.
I mean it is different than the boxing rings I've
seen, but somehow I can tell that that's what it
is.

I am startled by the blowing of horns. I
look to the rock shelf above the village and see
several men blasting cow horns.

Girls, about my age, are the first to
gather at the pits. They are wearing beads

swung over their shoulders and woven into bands of beautiful designs around their waists.

I take a deep breath. I look at Katie, then at Jeff. "Well?"

"It's now or never." Jeff says.

Katie closes the transmodulator and Jeff places it into its case on my back.

Chapter 4

We stand up and slowly make our way
out of the bushes. The village is now bustling.
People are gathering everywhere. There is a
polite hush as we wander through the crowd.
Like we could understand them even if they did
talk about us, but they say nothing.

Please Babo, just notice us and let's go, I
think.

As I look around at these people in their
world so obviously different from mine – I
notice how very much the same we all seem to
be. Girls are admiring each other's hair.
Mothers are tidying young children. Fathers
are encouraging their wrestler sons. And
young men and young women are making
googlie-eyes at each other.

Katie nudges me and points to a boy who is staring at us. I pull out the photo I'd printed from the transmodulator.

It is Babo all right.

I smile and wave. The boy grins broadly and breaks away from his group. He is dressed like one of the wrestlers.

"Babo?" I ask.

He extends his hand in western fashion. Jeff takes it. The boys shake. Odd that he know this gesture...but then he knows many rescue workers and attended a western-type school.

"Hello," Katie smiles warmly.

Babo is long and lean, but his face is very young. He is oiled and glistening in the sun. He is ready for a match – or so it seems.

"Hi," Babo speaks in broken English, "are you Phinus?"

"I'm Phineas," I move forward. "These are my friends Jeff and Katie. Are you Babo?"

"I am Babo. Are we to go?" His English is slow and practiced. I can't help but think that too much western stuff is going to ruin this wonderful culture.

What a great place this village is. Here we were, three white kids and nobody even cares. Or at least they don't gawk at how different we look from them.

And, everyone's so happy. They are all laughing and smiling and partying. This seems like more than just a sporting event – this seems like a celebration of some kind.

"We are to go." Katie says, reaching for the transmodulator.

"Wait," I turn and move the backpack out of her reach. I look at Babo. "Are you fighting?"

"Wrestling," he corrects. "Yes, but now we go."

"No, we'll watch and then we'll go." I said. I purposely do not look at Katie. I just know she's shooting me dirty looks. You know, the kind that would kill you if they ever got the chance.

Soon, stretched around the wrestling ring are pairs of fighters. They square off with one another. They dance around each other – sizing one another up – for over five minutes. Around and around each other they walk. Finally, the first pair enter the ring.

I am getting nervous. I feel like it's important for Babo to have his last wrestle, but with the way it went in Sierra Leone, part of me wants to get going home while the going is good. The second pair enters the ring.

I rub the remote belt around my waist. I feel better knowing that with the push of a button – I can be home.

The match is more than just wrestling. Babo explains that they are celebrating a good harvest and that it is an honor to wrestle. He looks sad – like this is the last time he'll ever get to participate in such an event. Actually, it probably is the last time he'll get to participate in such and event – at least for a while.

I learn something very interesting about these people – something that I plan to remember and take back to our new International Coalition of Children for Peace. I learn that these people of the Nuba Mountains are not wrestling for prizes or fame or anything that we would be wresting for at home. They're just wrestling because it's a tradition and because it's fun – nothing more – nothing less.

It dawns on me that these are the very

reasons why my family does some of the things we do -- things like putting up a Christmas tree in December or watching the town parade on the Fourth of July. We do these things because they are fun and because they are traditions.

These are not the same reasons why I play soccer or go to swim meets. I do those things to win. So do my friends. We do them because winners are cool and popular and can grow up to make tons of money – not because they are fun or traditional.

If the truth be known, sometimes I hate soccer...sometimes I would rather just be riding my bike, but then the winning thing creeps up in me and the thought that if I do really well I might end up in the paper. These last reasons don't seem to exist here. Maybe I have it wrong. I begin to feel that I know nothing about what it means to do something for the sport of it.

And, if I'm not already feeling too competitive – I learn that these people of the Nuba Mountains participate in such events to strengthen their sense of community. You know, that home feeling people get from working together – bonding-like. Wouldn't my coach love to hear me know? Let's not worry about winning coach – let's just all bond and get along. Yeah, that would go over really well.

I do notice, however, that some things are universal – you know, the same everywhere. Like the best sportsman gets the prettiest girls. This is obvious as these prettiest girls are flocking around the rings and following the victors. Figures. I guess that popularity is popularity no matter where you are.

Babo is about to start. He and his opponent look like they are around the same age, but the other boy is bigger, scarier.

For over twenty minutes the two are locked in combat. It is a close match, but Babo wins. His tribe surrounds him. Girls start taking off their beads and putting them around his neck. Other kids, about our age, hoist him onto their shoulders and take him on a victory walk around the ring.

Katie nudges me. It is her 'we need to go nudge'.

I'm thinking the same thing.

I look around for Jeff – who is off with Babo and some of the other boys their age – whooping up the victory.

"It'll be dark soon," I answer her silent plea to leave.

"I don't want to be here after dark." Katie looks up at the sky.

The sun has faded into a dull gray and the dusk suddenly seems still and quiet.

"There's something stirring in the forest."

Katie indicates a spot beyond the village. A spot beyond the protection of the rocks.

I look but see nothing. "You're just freaking yourself out," I say, but a chill runs through me and I can't help but feel that maybe she's right.

Chapter 5

Jeff and Babo and their cheering, celebrating crew are well down the trail and almost in the center of the village before we catch up. I look at Jeff, who is obviously having a great time. He has that "we just won the championship" look in his eyes – and pow! – it hits me how amazing people are.

Then another thought hits me. That maybe, just maybe, people wouldn't fight or carry on or have so many wars or "conflicts" if our leaders would just let us be the leaders.

No, really, I think I'm on to something. Here we are in this remote part of the world, with people who do not even know what television is, and they are being so nice to us. And, I like them. I like them and I can't even talk to most of them. Some can speak English, some are speaking what sounds like Arabic, but most are speaking what must be a tribal language. Only none of that matters. The boys are treating Jeff like he is one of their own and the girls are smiling at Katie and me. Maybe, just maybe, grown-ups would have an easier if they didn't make everything so complicated. If, just every once in a while, they let themselves act like carefree kids.

Jeff bounces over. "They are celebrating their harvest. They want us to join in their feast."

"Cool!" I say, before remembering that we really should go. It's part of the carefree kid thing – why go when there is celebrating to be had?

I'm torn. Katie's bush boogie man is still in the back of my mind, but what an experience spending a little more time with these people will be. Besides, I'm really hungry. We haven't eaten in hours.

"Phinney, we need to go." Katie looks at Jeff and amps her tone. "Now!"

"Ah, lighten up Kate!" Jeff says good-naturedly. "Just think of all you could learn about these people."

Katie pauses for a moment. I think he has her. Dangle learning in front of Katie and you almost always have a sold deal.

"Forty-five minutes. No more," she reluctantly agrees.

"Deal," we all say at the same time, piling our hands on top of one another. "Break!"

Jeff runs to catch up with Babo and the others. Several girls, around our age, trail back. One speaks English. "I am Salif."

I smile as Katie and I move to walk on the other side of Salif as we head into one of the compounds under the giant canopy rock. "I'm Phineas and this is Katie."

Her smile dances into an infectious laugh. "Phineas? What a funny name."

We can't help but laugh with her. She has one of those laughs. You know the kind that just makes your stomach tickle and your chest feel like it's going to burst. "I guess it is kind of funny."

"You will join us for eating? We are having sorghum and fresh maize cobs roasted on the fire."

Maize I figure is corn. Sorghum...I have no idea.

"It sounds wonderful," I say and Katie nods a smile, but she's looking around. She is still nervous. I let Salif get a little ahead of us. "It's ok Katie. Relax." I grab my best friend's hand. "These are nice people."

"It isn't them I'm worried about. It's the Mujahedin." Now, I look around. It all seems quiet.

Salif comes back to us. She takes Katie's hand in a gesture of friendship. The laughter is gone from her eyes. "Katie, they have not come for many harvests."

"Oh, I'm sorry," Katie apologizes, embarrassed that Salif heard her comment. "I didn't mean anything by it."

"You do not need sorry. I was a young girl when they last came. Before I began the missionary school. Before I began the Arab school. My mum hid me. We survived in a burning sal. The wrestler who won the last match of the day, Babo, he lost his entire family. So did many others. Babo's sisters and brothers were taken and his parents were killed."

The sorrow in my eyes can't begin to come close to matching hers. "How sad."

"Very. I did not sleep for many darknesses. Sometimes I still have nightmares.

But my father says we cannot live in fear of them. He says this is almost as bad as being taken by them."

"I guess, either way they win." Katie says.

"Win?" Salif does not know the word.

"Nothing," I say, smiling. We are inside one of the compounds now.

"Let's eat," Salif resumes her light mood and bounds towards the flickering firelight inside the circular hut.

I look at Katie. "Can you imagine what it must have been like?"

Katie shutters. "I don't even want to think about it."

The men are ushered into one hut, the holua, to eat. We will eat in the main hut with the women.

The sorghum is a sweet mush. We enjoy it as the women tell stories. The young children stare at us.

"They have never seen the Hawajas." The woman who is cooking explains.

"What is Hawajas?" Katie looks at Salif, who is seated between us, and asks softly.

"Hawaja is someone from far away. A different land. Light like you." Salif answers. "When I was very young we were without food. One day trunks pulled up and began to unload big sacks of lentils and sorghum seeds, barrels of oil for cooking, blankets and medicine. My father told me that the Hawajas are good people, like you." She smiles. "They had come from far away because the rains had failed."

A grandmotherly lady leans over to us. "They came many times that year. I fear what would have happened had they not. But the

Arabs, who share our own country, did not help us. They do not help us."

The lady smiles sweetly. She is missing teeth and she has scars all over her body. I read about the scars before I came. They are "kell" or signs of beauty. Many of the older women have them, but none of the younger ones do. While it is still thought to be beautiful scarring isn't practiced anymore. It is too painful. It is too old-fashioned.

I look out of the door and notice that dusk has turned to night. The red sky is completely black now and stars twinkle all around.

Dinner is over and the men begin to filter into the hut. One of them stands before the crowd and starts to tell a story. I can't understand him, but his gestures and tone are so elaborate, or big, I can tell it must be a whopper. And the people around me are laughing, but then laughter begins to fade.

I look at my watch. It is way past midnight. We need to go.

We have been asked to stay many times by many people. They are confused as to how we got here. They are confused as to why we came. They don't say anything though – they just suggest that the three Hawaja children stay in the safety of their village until morning. Only, somehow I feel that the safety is slipping away. The laughter has died and the villagers seem to be listening to something ...listening to something I can't hear.

I look at Katie. "Let's find Jeff and Babo and go home."

"I'm with you."

The room is quiet now, uncomfortably quiet. If I strain I think I can hear shouting in the distance. Nervously, I reach for the remote.

I breathe easier knowing that it is still there. I grab Katie's hand.

"Let's find Jeff and get outta here," I say, but it is too late.

Chapter 6

I can hear noises now – muffled shouting noises and they are getting closer. They are chaotic and frantic and they make the hair stand up on the back of my neck.

The Nuba around us seem to be frozen. The man telling the story moves to the door and opens it. There are flames coming from the far end of the village. An amber glow dances in the night.

This is new to me and doesn't register at first. But then I see and suddenly the sounds make sense. Fire! The entire south end of the village is ablaze – burning ambers are spitting from the grass roofs. The shouts are no longer distant and they have turned to frightened screams.

The night air has grown cold and a wind whirls into the hut. It is not freezing or anything, but I feel chilled to the bone. Ironically, I shiver as I stare into the fiery huts.

I move out the door with the rest of the people. I am still holding Katie's hand. Chaos is all around.

"Jeff!" I shout, pointing to the only other white person in the village.

"Babo's with him. Run!" Katie shouts.

We race in and out of the other people. People who are fleeing for their lives and the lives of their children.

"Mujahedin!" Yells a village elder. "Arab raiders are in our village."

I am in a nightmare – only I'm wide awake.

In the distance, people are racing through the village with torches. We watch as they set fire to one thatch hut roof after another. The people inside fly out and these men, the Mujahedin, pounce on them –

pounding them with their fists and then stabbing them with their knives.

I loose sight of Jeff and Babo as the man who was telling the story grabs my arm and pulls us up a trail deep into the hills. Raiders are everywhere, dragging people from their huts, slicing throats, and laughing – deep chesty laughs that hold no humor.

I have never seen a murder before. I have never seen the life bleed out of another. It is not something I ever wanted to see. It is sad and tragic and if I had time to think about it – I would probably be being throwing up about now. Only, I don't have time for that and all I can think about is getting away.

The smoke and the flames are surrounding us now – even as we head for the trail. Through the ashes and embers floating about in the air I catch sight of Jeff and Babo again. I try to scream, but no sound comes out.

I hear Katie gasp as we disappear into the trees. I turn to see Jeff and Babo – Jeff and Babo being dragged by the dirty, bearded Mujahedin.

Instinct takes over. I pull free from the kind man who is trying to rescue the foreign children.

All I have to do is touch Babo and get into remote range with Jeff. I can't let them be taken by these grungy, knife swinging men.

My legs are pounding. My feet are tripping over the rocks. I can't even breathe. I can tell that Katie is having trouble keeping up, but I will not slow down and I refuse to let go of her hand.

"The remote, Phineas, the remote!"

"We're not close enough!" I pant.

I watch as Jeff and Babo are tackled, dragged to their feet and led out of the village by the flickering light of the burning huts. I hear screams all around me. I see parents grabbing for children and children watching as parents are slashed with knives.

I realize how very different this part of the world is.

With Katie still close behind, we follow the man who has taken Jeff and Babo. The night air is cold and my lungs hurt from running.

"Phineas! Jeff, they took Jeff!" I look back and Katie is crying.

I stop, just for a minute. I realize that I am crying too. "We'll find them."

"Where are the missionaries?" She asks. "Where are the adults who are supposed to help us?"

"I think we're on our own this time," I say. "I don't think there are going to be any helpers."

"We can't leave them. Maybe we should get your Grandfather."

I take her by the shoulders. Her eyes reveal that she is as scared as I am. "It's us Katie. This is our mission. We have to do this. We have to follow them."

"Listen," she says straining to hear. "More horses. How are we going to keep up with horses?"

Gunfire breaks out behind us. Neither of us move. Life has just switched to slow motion. You know, like when you fall down or crash on your bike and things don't seem to be happening in real time. Instead they happen at an incredibly slow pace. It's like the universe wants you to feel the fear for as long as possible. Or maybe it's to give you time to think. Either way, it's like that now. The gunfire is like that – only in a paralyzing, terrorizing sort of way.

I look around frantically. I have no idea how we are going to keep up with horses. I only know that we have to try.

Chapter 7

The glow from the burning village is behind us, the dark and dangerous Nuba Mountains are around us, and the chaotic hoof prints loom in front of us.

Neither Katie nor I say a word as we follow the prints with only one flashlight. We can still hear the horses echo through the valleys and mountains. The crackling of the burning village has faded into the night, but the glow still illuminates the sky behind us.

We walk for over an hour before we can no longer hear the echo of the hooves or the crackling of the fire.

Then I see something. Katie does too. I can tell, because she stops.

"Phineas," she points to an orange glow.

"Do you think it's another village on fire?" I ask.

"It's too small, too controlled, maybe they set up camp or something."

We stop and listen. The air is still and chilly. I can't hear the horses anymore. Either they are too far ahead or they have stopped.

"There isn't any screaming and the fire looks little." Katie offers.

"Maybe you're right. Maybe they've just stopped."

We duck off the path and quietly move through the trees. We head towards the light. Slowly we creep. If we make a sound and are discovered – we're history.

I reach back and touch the transmodulator. It makes me feel safe.

As we move closer to what we can now see is an opening, we hear the muffled sounds of men speaking a foreign language.

"It's Arabic," Katie answers before I can ask. "Mujahedin means Arab raider. That's what that old man said."

"Do you see Jeff?" I look at the opening. I see Babo, but Jeff is no where in sight.

"No," Katie strains to see.

"Maybe he got away." I say.

"I don't see how."

"Maybe..." I can't finish what I am thinking because what I am thinking is just too scary.

"Phineas, don't even say it."

"Do you think one of us should circle around...get closer to those guys?"

"I wish I could speak Arabic."

"You know just about everything. How did you miss Arabic?" I force a smile. I am trying to make Katie feel better. Ever since her mom died when we were kids – I feel like it's my duty to protect Katie – to make her feel better. I am not doing such a hot job of that now.

There are four men guarding Babo and about twenty other kids.

I wish the transmodulator would let us take them all with us.

"Phineas," Katie interrupts my thoughts, "we need to leave Jeff."

"What!" I can't believe she'd even think it.

"Not leave, leave, but take Babo back and then get help to find Jeff."

"And how do you suppose we do that? Just march up, say excuse me and take Babo? You're out of your mind."

"Phineas, I'm serious. One of us stays with the transmodulator and one of us makes a run for Babo. If we leap at him and then the other presses the button when he's touched...poof...we're home."

"Katie," I say pointing to the belts worn by all of the raiders, "those are not toys they're wearing around their waists." I am referring to the pistol and dagger each man has tucked into a military-type belt.

"Do you have a better idea?"

I am silent.

"Do you?"

I hear something. It is coming from behind us.

"Well!?"

"Shhh, listen!" I whisper.

The ground is crackling and the trees and bushes are moving. Someone is approaching.

We've been discovered!

Katie hears it now too. I look around, but there is no escape route. I fumble for the remote belt. I pause. I look at Katie.

"We have to do it Phin. We have to."

I push the button but nothing happens. Nothing happens! Something's always supposed to happen! Grandpa promised! Where are the adults!?

"Hurry Phineas!" Katie urges in a frightened whisper.

"It won't work." I say without breathing. I can't breath. You know the feeling you get when the wind is knocked out of you…I have that now.

Katie looks at the belt. "That's the latch! Here." Katie reaches for the button but is stopped by a silent figure who grabs both of us at the same time. It covers our mouths. My breath is gone forever. I just know it.

"Shhhhhh!" The familiar voice hisses as he rips our heads around to face him.

My breath returns.

"Jeff!" I sigh

"Jeff!" Katie echoes my sigh.

We hug – long and hard and good.

"How did you get here?" I ask.

"We saw them take you away. He grabbed you and Babo, put you on his horse." Katie adds.

"He did take me, but he couldn't hold both of us on his horse. We were galloping through the forest, at full speed, and we caught up to his friends. We stopped and they started talking about me being white."

"How do you know what they were saying?" I ask. Jeff does not speak Arabic. Jeff barely speaks English.

"Babo goes to an Arab school now. Most of the Christian missionaries left because of this war that's going on – that's not really going on. See, it isn't an official war so…"

"Jeff!" I stop him. "Get to the point."

"Ok, ok. So, we stop and these guys

start talking about the trouble they'd be in because they have an American or British kid."

"How did they know where you're from?" I interrupt again.

"Because I can't keep my mouth shut." He shoots me a dirty look. Maybe I won't ask anymore questions until he's done. "So they're talking and Babo tells me that I have to do something because they're pretty much going to slit my throat." He makes an exaggerated gesture with his hand – you know the slicing your throat kind – only in this situation it does not seem so very exaggerated. "While they were talking – I slid off of the horse and made my way back to the village."

"They just let you go?" Katie asks and I guess it's ok for her to ask questions because she doesn't get a dirty look.

"It was dark and they didn't want me. I don't know. Maybe they figured I wasn't worth it."

"Long story short, I find a village elder. Actually, he finds me and tells me that these kids have been taken to be sold into slavery -- in Khartoum and other places. Khartoum is the capital of Sudan. And these Arab raiders sell them to other Arabs there – literally for slaves – just like I heard on the radio."

"It's so sad. They'll never see their families again." I say.

"Yeah, it's tragic...but we need to get Babo and go home." Katie says.

"We can't just let all those kids be...be." I can't even say what could happen to them.

"Our best chance to help them is to go back and talk to Grandpa Clooney," Katie says, and I know she is right, only I can't leave.

A cloud of dust rises seconds before the sound of horses reach my ears.

"Crud! They're moving again." I say.

"Come on!" Jeff enters the clearing as the last horse leaves.

I jump up and follow. Katie sighs – having no choice but to do the same.

Chapter 8

It's almost dawn. We can't hear the horses anymore, but we are still following their tracks. The Nuba Mountains have flattened out into dry desert land.

We approach a town. The horses seem to have skirted the edge of it – riding around rather than through. We do the same. It is noon before we finally reach the end of the trail. I can smell the horses. We are at a camp with about thirty green army-like tents tucked behind a huge cyclone fence. You know the kind that usually surrounds schools or playgrounds. The city we circled looms in the background.

"Look," Katie points.

We catch a glimpse of a group of girls heading into what looks like a livestock shower stall. It is long and cement with faucets sticking out of a block wall.

"Do you see Babo?" Jeff asks.

"He's got to be in one of those tents." I point to the only two tents being guarded. "See the guards?"

"Of course, we wouldn't want them to lose any of their precious booty." Jeff says sarcastically. It strikes a nerve in me that he calls these people 'booty', like they are nothing more than cargo or stuff – inanimate things to be bought and sold. Inanimate is a word my social science teacher likes to use for things that aren't alive. Like King Arthur's sword was an inanimate object; however, it decided who would be the king.

The way Jeff refers to them makes me more determined than ever to help them – and not just Babo – all of them.

"So, Phineas, do we have a plan?" Katie asks. She looks as tired as I feel and as hungry. I realize that we haven't eaten since dinner last night.

Of course, instantly I feel guilty for thinking about eating when those poor kids have just lost their futures.

"I guess we wait until night time, sneak into the tent and transmodulate out." I say.

"Sounds easy, but how are we going to get past the guards?" Jeff asks.

"I don't know. I didn't even have a plan until two seconds ago." I defend.

"Maybe they'll come out."

So, we wait and watch. The girls finish showering and are given what looks like clean shirts to put on. They hang like dresses and make the girls look even younger – sadder.

We stir when two cars pull up. They look shiny and new.

"What do you think they want?" Jeff asks.

"Shhhh," Katie warns. The men in the cars are being escorted right past us. The bushes are not that thick and if they look close enough they could probably see us.

They stop. I can touch them without even straining. I look at Katie and then at Jeff. Neither of them is breathing either.

The men are talking – only it's the Arab thing again. Mental note, get one of those handheld language translators with an earphone. Get one of those handheld translators with an earphone if we ever get out of here – that is.

One of the guards brings a line of girls out of the tent and the men from the cars look them over. I mean look them over, look them over! Look them over like they are buying an animal...like these kids are nothing more than

88

merchandise. They poke and they pinch. They lift up the shirts the girls are wearing as dresses – inspecting everywhere.

Then it hits me. To these men the girls *are* animals, slaves...not human. I clench my fists. It takes everything I have inside not to run out there and demand that they stop. I want to scream at the top of my lungs: "They are little girls you morons! Leave them alone!"

Of course if I do – I'll be spending forever living in a basement and slaving for other people, too. My only chance to help them is by getting home and working with this committee Grandpa Clooney is assembling.

I look at the faces of the little girls. I have never seen such terror in anyone's eyes. The oldest is probably ten...the youngest five. I keep hoping I'll wake up and when I tell Grandpa Clooney about this nightmare – he'll laugh and say: "Oh, Phinney, you and your imagination. That could never happen."

Only it is happening.

The men settle on a whimpering girl about six. She is sucking her thumb and refuses to let go of a slightly older girl. They look alike. They are probably sisters. They finally pry the purchased one away. Her tears turn silent as she is carried into the car. The others stare after her. They look as numb as I feel as the car drives out of sight leaving only a trail of dust.

Numb and frightened. I could not imagine being them.

Not Katie or Jeff or I say a word. We just sit and watch and wait until night. The time passes slowly. It is hot and I'm hungry, but mostly I'm sick. Sick because there are more cars that pull up. Sick because the cars pulling up are full of well-dressed men –

business looking men – only their business seems to be brutalizing children.

I, Phineas J. Clooney, am witnessing something I never dreamed possible. I, Phineas J. Clooney, have lived a very sheltered life. And I want to be sheltered again. But I can't. Not ever again, because now I have seen too much – because, now I have to make a difference.

I think of all of the secret agents I've ever heard of before. James Bond surfaces as my favorite. I wonder if James Bond ever missed his mom? I sure miss mine.

Finally, the camp quiets down. The air turns cold again. I look at my watch. It is well past midnight.

"It's now or never guys." I say.

"Give me the transmodulator," Katie says, "you guys run faster. Jeff you sneak into the tent. I've been watching. See that corner over there?" Katie points to the back corner closest to us. "It's loose. A kid's been poking his head out all day. You can probably squeeze under." She turns to me. "When he's under, Phineas, you run about halfway between me and the tent. Jeff, you need to scream when you're touching Babo."

"Then I'll push the remote. If I'm halfway between the transmodulator and you Jeff – it'll work on all of us." I add.

Katie takes out the transmodulator and fires it up.

"Ready?" I ask.

Katie nods. Jeff sneaks away towards the tent.

We watch as he crawls under the green flap without any trouble. When his feet disappear I run to my spot in the center between him and Katie.

I wait for the scream. I wait for the scream.

But the scream comes from me! It comes from me as I am blinded by a flashlight and grabbed from behind. It happens so fast that I can't push the remote.

I am in big trouble.

Chapter 9

I kick and scream. I struggle to get free.
Katie runs from out of the bushes –
transmodulator in hand.

"Push the button!" She yells.

"I can't reach it!" I panic. "Use the red
one on the transmodulator."

We hear Jeff's signal.

I am biting and wiggling and frantically
trying to get away!

"I'm an American!" I yell. "You can't do
this to me. I have rights. Those kids have
rights."

I give one hard kick and am free.   "Now!"
I yell to Katie.

Katie pushes the button – as the belt
falls from my waist. It must have come loose in
the fight.

I watch as Katie vanishes. I hear the surprised screams come from the tent and can only imagine that Jeff and Babo have disappeared as well.

I am all alone and captive in Africa. Suddenly, I am one of those frightened little girls.

I manage to grab my belt and shove it into my pants as I am whisked up and carried into another tent.

There is a lantern on a metal desk. A bearded man sits behind it. He is dark and dirty and it smells inside. It smells like dirt and sweat and grime. It smells sticky and sweet and I have to swallow hard not to gag.

The man holding onto me shouts something to the other. Their words sound angry. The man behind the desk glares at me – shouting.

I say nothing. How can I answer when I have no idea what he is saying?

Please come back Jeff and Katie...please!

I hear a word that sounds like American in the guttered, mumbled conversation of my captors.

"Who are you?" The desk-man asks – his voice low and angry.

Why is it that someone anywhere can always speak English? Granted his accent is horrible and I barely understand him – but it is English – sort of.

"I am an American and I demand that you let all of these children go!"

The man raises his eyebrows. He sits back and laughs. "Oh, you do do you?" He turns to my guard and mumbles something and with an angry gesture of his hand I am taken from the room and put in the tent with the other girls.

They are from the village. I recognize many from the wrestling match. They are young...too young to have gone to a missionary school. Too young to know English. They are kind. They try to comfort me.

"Taja," a girl about five indicates her name.

"Phineas," I say as she crawls on my lap and fades off to sleep.

Maybe they think I am here to save them? Great, I'll save them – only who's going to save me?

I drift into a fitful sleep.

I wake up at dawn as we are being pulled out of the tent and shoved onto the back of two pickup trucks beyond the gate of the camp.

Babo is already in the back of the truck. He nods at me but does not say a word. He indicates with his eyes that we are being watched. I bite my lip and take a seat near Taja.

We set off. The ride is rough as we bump down the road. We come to a crossing and turn onto a larger road. It's still dirt but the ride is much smoother.

I pray that the tracking device in my remote belt is working and that Katie and Jeff...better yet...that my Grandpa...will be rescuing me any minute now.

We come to a river. It is the rainy season and the river is high and raging. I stand.

Taja points to the man in the front and to the rearview mirror. I smile at her and motion for her to stay down.

The truck is going about thirty miles per hour. I think about the time Katie and I flew through the air when we raced off the cliff in our go-cart. We were probably going this fast. And we fell far. It didn't hurt that bad.

I look ahead. We are the final truck.
Babo moves closer.

"We have to jump," I say quietly. "It's our
only chance."

"They'll see us." He says.

"Maybe...maybe not." I say.

"But if they catch us..." his voice trails
off.

"They'll what...capture us and sell us
into slavery...oh, wait...they're doing that now."
I say. "Come on!"

I pull him to his feet, take one last look
at our driver, and jump out of the back of the
truck. Babo follows and we roll down into the
roaring waters of the river below.

Chapter 10

The current takes me under. I'm tumbling and rolling in the rushing river. I can't tell which way to swim. I look for the light of the sky, but everything is dark. I watch for the bubbles to rise, but they are swirling all around me.

I remember to stop, to be still. The current is pulling me, but I manage to float to the top. I cough and spit out the cold water. My lungs feel heavy. I see Babo churning up ahead.

"Babo," I choke. "Babo!" My voice is stronger and he hears. He raises a hand but he cannot turn.

The river thrusts me towards the shore. My heart sinks. The trucks have stopped and the men are pointing their pistols.

This is not good.

"Babo! Guns!" I yell as I duck under the water – as if it can protect me from the bullets that are raining on us.

Babo has reached a calmer section of the river and is swimming to the other side. "Over here," he calls.

The men are running along the bank...still firing.

I reach Babo, as they are reloading.

"Hurry!" Babo yells as he pulls me – still choking – into the trees of his Nuba foothills.

Gunfire echoes across the valley and up into the mountains. We run, higher, faster. The gunfire fades. It stops all together. We hear the engines start up.

"No one ever makes it back," Babo says.

"They take them so young – who would try to escape?" I say.

"I am not young." Babo says. "But I was scared and the horse we were in."

"It's called a truck." I say. I realize that Babo had never seen a truck before, let alone driven in one.

"It was fast. I was dizzy. I would never have jumped." He says.

"That's what they count on. Your fear and the fact that your world is so different from there's." I look around. "Any idea where we are?"

"Of course, my father and I use to take our cows to graze in that pasture." A sad shadow clouds his eyes. "That is why my parents were killed. So they can take children. They teach us to fear the raider, they tell us about the killing but not about the other things." He says.

"You mean the slavery?"

Babo looks lost. I don't think he really knows what is going to happen to his friends...what almost happened to him.

"Phineas," he says. "Listen."

We stand still, silent. I hear nothing at first – but then I hear footsteps swish the trees and crunch the ground.

"Too heavy for my people," Babo says. "Raiders!"

He's right. The Nuba go barefoot and barely make any noise.

I move to take cover behind a bush but the footsteps are upon us.

In one move, I am tackled and taken to the ground. I see Babo fall beside me.

I am swirling again, like I'm in the river only it's not cold. My stomach turns. I'm falling, falling, falling.

I land in a thump...on the floor of the candy factory...on top of Jeff and Katie and a startled Babo.

I run to Grandpa Clooney's arms.

Jeff helps a confused and frightened Babo up. He puts his arms around our new friend. "Let's get something to eat and I'll explain everything."

He takes Babo out of the office.

"How did you find me?" I ask as Katie joins our embrace.

"I'm sorry we left you."

"The belt fell off right as you were pushing the button. I thought I'd never get out!"

"Whoa, girls! What are you talking about?" Grandpa asks.

It hits me that Grandpa doesn't know we were separated and that his princess was almost slave-meat.

"We had a plan and my belt dropped," I begin.

"Just when I was pushing the transmodulator because Phineas couldn't get to the remote."

"She and Jeff disappeared and I was almost sold into slavery."

"But we came back for her. We tracked her with the homing device – only we lost her."

"The river!" The water must have messed with the transmission.

"The river," Katie repeats, "we figured that the device had to have gotten wet, or something, to stop working."

"After we transmodulated home we went directly back and hid in those same bushes Phineas." Katie says. "When the trucks took you away – we followed – only we ended up on the other side of the river because we didn't want the raiders to see us. When you disappeared off the screen we figured you made a getaway into the river."

"Then you found us." Phineas says.

"I think I need it slower," Grandpa said. "But first, what do you say we join Jeff and Babo and Saramba for a little lunch and a long talk?"

Grandpa hugs us both close and we venture off down the hallway to the first unofficial meeting of the International Coalition of Children for Peace.

THE TOP SECRET FILES
OF
PHINEAS J. CLOONEY

TOPIC – SUDAN

PROCEED WITH CAUTION

Chapter 11

More on the Sudan

Different Region – More Tragic Stuff

Hey, Phineas here again. We just finished our briefing with Grandpa and his group of suited, sunglassed co-workers...not the candy kind...they wear white...but the agent kind...who are darker and never, ever smile.

See, every time we come back from an assignment we have to sit down and tell them about everything that happened. And I mean everything! Then they ask a ton of questions and we have to answer them – over and over and over again.

Today, Saramba was there. It was great to see her. She looked so happy. She can't wait until she's ready to go on an assignment like us.

Anyway, after we talked and the suited guys asked their questions – they told us some more things about the Sudan. It seems that the things going on in the Nuba Mountains, where we just came from, are only the beginning of a long and sad story that makes me very, very angry!

Ok, there's this place called the Darfur region also in the Sudan – kind of down and left of the Nuba Mountains if you were to look at a map. Anyway, talking about this Darfur region, I learned a word that is sadder, more tragic and much scarier than slavery. The word is genocide. Genocide is a word that I wish I had never heard, now or in my whole entire life left to go.

Genocide means that one group of people makes a plan and carefully goes about killing an entire other group of people – on purpose! That's right. One group just up and decides it is better than another and they work at weakening and killing this other selected, unlucky, group. And I mean the entire other group...as in all of the people who belong to that particular ethnicity, religion or tribe...no exceptions! Goal – total elimination.

The African Sudanese are the ones who are being killed. A group of government-backed Arab militias are the ones who are killing. In other words, these government-backed Arab militias are the ones practicing genocide.

See, the same government in Khartoum – the capital of Sudan – who are letting the raiders kidnap people and sell them into slavery – are the ones who are paying the militias to kill the people who were originally in the Sudan. The African Sudanese...the ones who where in the country first, the quiet people who where so nice to us and who are so willing to share with us...are the ones being victimized.

Of course, the government denies any involvement – only all of the evidence (and evidence is mounting and mounting) points to the fact that this government is helping. I, personally, think that their goal is to get rid of all of the African Sudanese – except the ones they can enslave – and take over the entire country. I mean, I'm just a kid and I can see this.

Grandpa told us about another boy our age who is the only survivor of his entire village, of like, two hundred people. This poor kid came home from school one day and saw his whole, entire village burning – just like we saw Babo's burning – only there weren't just a few Arab raiders (like the ones who captured us) but many Arab raiders on horseback surrounding the village and killing everyone in

it. They call them the Arab Janjaweed militia
and they are ruthless.

These Janjaweed's have made more than
a million, yes I said million, innocent people,
flee their villages. And an organization called
the Human Rights Watch says that more than
10,000 people have been killed in the past year
or so. Some people say that this number is too
low – that maybe as many as 30,000 people
were killed. Now! This year! Not a hundred
years ago, but now.

A group called the Human Rights Watch
has tons of stuff on the details of these horrible
things going on in the Sudan. So does a
different group called Amnesty International.
You can find both of them online. It is
interesting to read. Ask an adult or older
brother or sister or someone to help you sort
through them. Some of it is hard to read, but
there are real stories from real people who are

victims. There are pictures too. It is almost too sad to look at – sad but worthwhile because the pictures and the stories make it more real and urgent and it needs to be urgent so we can get the adults to do something about it.

You can also read more about "genocide" – trying to kill an entire race of people or the people of an entire religion – on my website www.adventuresinreading.com.

Anyway, Grandpa says that Darfur is going to get even more tragic and we need to do something now – before it's too late.

Oh, and get this – not only is the Sudanese government helping this militia, but they aren't letting aid in to the refugees who have been forced out of their homes.

See, not all of the people who are terrorized, not all of the people forced out of their villages, die. They live – only they don't have homes to go back too so they wander around. They wander around homeless and foodless and then they starve to death under the hot African sun. I know that sometimes I exaggerate, but I'm not this time. They are really dying.

The lucky ones, the ones who don't die right away, end up in places called refugee camps. A refugee is a person who flees someplace, usually his or her country, in search of safety. Aid organizations or just ordinary people set up places, usually tent cities if people are lucky, so that the people who need it can get food and water and medicine.

Only in Darfur the people aren't getting enough help and the government won't let outsiders in to set up these camps.

That's right, the government is making things worse. Grandpa knows another boy who was playing ball when government...

government...planes firebombed the kid's village. Then they killed the adults and stole the little girls.

After our time in the Nuba Mountains – we know what is going to happen to them. I'm not sure which is worse...a lifetime of slavery or dying in a firebomb. Neither sounds desirable to this American kid.

What Grandpa told me makes me mad...really mad! I am so mad – I have to do something, only I'm not sure what at this point. There are about 80 tribes in this particular part of the Sudan and Grandpa says that it is the goal of the bad people to get rid of them all.

The refugees who get out tell stories of mass murders. A mass murder is when groups of people are killed. Mass Murder – in this case is genocide.

Grandpa told us about the land that these Janjaweed are taking. It's about the size of California and has little water or industry and no electricity. The African tribes used to live peacefully, but now in the summer, when it rains a lot, the Arabs south of Darfur come into Darfur to get away from the bugs and mosquitoes and they don't want to share with the people who've lived there for, like, ever. There's a drought in the north so these Arabs are moving south – farther into the Darfur region. This means the Sudanese are being squished in the middle.

These Arabs are nomadic – in other words, they move around a lot, but the Africans in Darfur are farmers or villagers who just stay put.

Before, like years past, leaders on both sides would sit down and talk about which routes the nomads would take without bothering the homes of the African Sudanese who live there. This seems really unfair. I know I wouldn't like anyone just bringing his cows into my backyard, setting up a tent and staying until the rain comes back to where he's from.

The negotiations, or talks, used to help these people get along by each giving in a little on both side, you know compromising – only talking isn't working anymore.

Some people think that the negotiations have failed because there is a record breaking drought going on and the desert is getting bigger and bigger. This means that the already extremely limited resources are getting less and less. Each year the nomads, who have cows and are looking for food, have to move farther into Darfur. In 2003, the Africans in Darfur spoke up because more and more of their land was being taken. The government in the capital sided with the Arabs.

See, the government, in Khartoum, is headed and run by very rich and very powerful Arab farmers and plantation owners, so, of course, they sided with their own people.

In April, a cease-fire was signed. And, as we know from our last little escapade, cease fires don't always work. Violence in Darfur is still raging and the Sudanese government won't let aid workers or doctors or reporters into the area to help. Basically, this part of the Sudan is closed off to the rest of the world and no one really knows exactly how bad it is. We only have stories from the refugees. It makes me shudder to even think about the horrible things going on there. Murder, starvation, slavery and worse!

The aid people who are there say that, basically, if the Sudanese government doesn't let them in to help the poor and starving and homeless people – if they are not able to set up refugee camps...that as many people will die as those who live in the entire state of Vermont.

For my next adventure check out...

www.adventuresinreading.com

You'll also find other great stories about the other Explorers and information about the people and events in this story.

Happy Reading.

Chapter 12

It is hard for me, Phineas J. Clooney, to believe that this is happening. As I go home and eat my dinner and watch a little television before I go to bed – it is hard to believe that at this very moment, somewhere far away, but still – somewhere on the same earth as me – there are people purposefully starving other people. It is hard to believe that groups of men on horseback are burning villages and killing people – over land that is only desert and because they happen to have different color skin than they do or because they believe in a different God than they do.

Here is what I am doing. I am writing my Senators and Congressmen. Heck, I'm even going to write the President of the United States and his wife. I figure that the President may be busy – but he'd never be too busy to listen to his wife and if we tell his wife about all that is going on – she's bound to care. President's wives are usually moms and moms care about these things.

Anyway, I'm going to tell them all that I care about the situation and that I want something done. I'm going to tell them that it makes me sad that our government only seems to help countries who have a lot of money or resources for money. I'm going to mention that it seems to me we only help people who have something that we want. I'm going to tell them that I don't care if we can get anything out of helping the African Sudanese – that we should help them just because they are people and they are in trouble...trouble is an understatement. They are dying...and it is our duty to help them.

I'm also going to tell my friends and my parents and I'm going to keep talking until someone listens.

Big breath...And, I'm going to raise money and make sure that it is used to buy stuff that will help the African Sudanese.

I hope I can get other kids to help me. I know we are, basically, only kids. We like to think we're tough and we like to pretend we're grown up, but when it comes down to it – most of us expect others to take care of us. Not that there is anything wrong with this. We *are* kids and we do need help. Heck, I actually like being a kid and I like depending on my parents and grandparents and teachers and stuff. But we are more that just kids. We are free kids who have a voice. We are free kids who can help those who can't help themselves. If not us – who? If not now – when?

We are kids who matter and we are kids who can make a difference – it's our job to show this to others. So, write a letter, start a petition drive by getting a bunch of your friends to sign a letter to the government saying that you'd like them to help these poor people, tell all of your friends what is going on.   Write the leaders of the United Nations and the Sudanese President. Tell them how mad you are and how we really have to help these people.

Make a difference! It's the most important thing you may do in the whole entire rest of your life.

The bad things that are happening are not movies or television shows or video games, but real pain and death happening to real people. We have two choices here. We can either: sit back and let it happen -- or we can help try to make it go away.

The choice is ours individually. I know what I'm going to do.

I'm Phineas J. Clooney, and I'm going to make a difference.

ISBN 1412039192-3

1402789